A WALK BACK HOME

VEDANSHI .S

"To my little champs Aarav ,Rayn and Siddhart I hope when you grow up read this you are proud of me'"

Contents

Acknowledgements

For the people who understood the literary popstar in me .
You know who you are ,just know I am thankful.

To Hancy who read my first literary work , your
reaction is the reason I reached so far . To my sisters ,Riya
and Vidushi who will probably never read this. To Hunar ,
thankyou for sticking through .

Lastly to all the people who told me I could reach
nowhere thankyou for keeping the drive in me alive.

1

The Art of being a keeper

—♡—

♡♡♡

When things don't work out, sit down and talk

this world has seen far many heart breaks from misunderstanding

than from infidelity.

Dont let them disrespect you but let not your ego wear facade of self respect.

People who love you will keep you but sometimes you have to be a keeper.

Trust me it would not be easy human beings never are.

Love is not a disney movie neither is it a rose full of thorns.

It is the harsh reality of life.

Don't let these movies convince you otherwise.

2

Misfit

"Walking on the grass letting the moist dew seep through my feet as I travelled a few miles ,

agitation swept through me. Making me shudder. One look at me and you could have tell

I wasn't thinking something that was pleasant to think of .

Counting the clavs of my finger imparting to my brain that we faced this together not

less than a week ago .Was it agonising for you? To slow perhaps ,were you bored by my suffering

or did it filled your heart with pity? for me it was an achievement stopping myself the millionth time.

I turned back and I left .I was high on optimism today to a point that edges of broad railing with droplets of rain seemed grass, green lush grass. The rain drops sat on the railing as I stood in this world it never mixed

never belong till it dries, till it dies."

I folded the letter tucked it neatly in the vintage envelope with stamps on it. I looked up in the mirror and a pair of teary eyes looked back at me. I did not knew who wrote that letter but what I knew was that person did not deserve pity but a hug filled with all gentle accords .

The letter was old and rusted maybe it was written years ago or maybe just a moment back.

The timeline of the letter did not intrigued me but it was the fact how beautifully someone had tucked all

their insecurities with utmost care and enclosed it in an envelope it was as if that envelope was the only barrier between my soul and a clustered mind .

On looking closely the stamps read 1907 . Perhaps it was written a century ago . It wasn't a letter it was a proof of collective failures of generations to come. It was a story of a misfit read by another.

3
Beauty of contrast

There is only one way you can spell love and yet a thousand ways you can define it.

It transends every person who said 'I could not have love them more'.

For some love is a reason for their revival ,the only reason for their survival

Love is sitting in a room with a person in eerie silence and finding solitude.

Love is burning the world for them. Love is taking a step back because they said so

Love is writing an epitaph even though every carve on that stone feels like it would forever be engraved in your heart

Love is the hands that touch you when they walk past the smile when you hear a name

Love is the person you see grow up from generational traumas or for some the person that felt home after so long.

From all the poems written on unrequited love there are so few on the pain of being the object of that affection.

So when you say love is collateral damage to heart know for some of us it is a chance for survival a last drop of revival.

4

Nostalgia

This futile sensation gets to me
A dreading feeling is all I see
I have lost my childhood,I have lost my childhood to it
I was so well protected wishing I would grow up fast
I had never been so wrong never been so wrong about something
So children go out there go out there and live
Till they let you ,till they tell you to be so consumed by your future that you forget to live
They say you are shaped in what you are when you are children.why do they have to fit us in moulds when we are mere infants
So be unapologetic and happy until your pillows are wet and I am fine is your catchphrase
Find beauty in this world until you have to get high to escape reality
Growing up is futile and sometimes nothing can take you back to the good old days.........

5

Inside a Grieving heart

I will tell you what it feels like to lose a person you love

No I won't use the word pain it is too small an adjective to describe the hollow feeling in the pit of your stomach the excuriating suffering in your head

It is feeling like home when you look at that ceiling of your room.It is looking at it for hours without blinking.

It is loosing your sleep ,and then using all your power to wake up.

It is the tormenting feeling when you are asked to leave the bed

It is loosing your apetite and eventually your will to go through each day

It is standing on the skyscrapers and looking down as the careless world walk by

It is the will of taking a step back
It is the story of gaining back power over your own life

It is looking yourself in the mirror and knowing there was nothing to love about you

It is knowing how easily replaceable you are

But most importantly it is knowing you would never be the same again.

6

The brightest star

Sit and stare at the stars know where you belong , where you belong in this universe

Like a star that shine so bright it takes up the whole sky be that person in someone's life

Lay if you must, close your eyes and think how presumptuous this world full of people is

Walk and run and stand tall but know that your opinion is irrelevant for many of us .

Be that girl that takes a lot of space and know that your wit is your most important armour

But most importantly know that you don't owe any man pretty , not atleast the one who thought you were beautiful just because of that

7

Courage

Violence to me is an act of cowardice.The same weapon a man choose a thousand years ago for he knew a girl with wits will outpower him

For no matter how much you try to defame him it takes a great deal of courage to be Mahatma Gandhi and only a revolver to be Nathuram Godse

It takes a great deal of courage to hold a knife to your throat and say you would do that a thousand times over for your country. It takes courage to pick up a pen and write when everybody is so interested in web woven lies .It takes a great deal of courage to say you stand with human rights and keeping your ground when those rights are not all that convenient.

So don't preach me about darkness for I have lived in it for far too long, Don't tell me I don't know how it feels cause I know better than anyone else ever could. Let me tell you what it takes it takes courage to look yourself in the mirror and not find anything to love about , it takes courage to wake up every morning and tell my mind that just this day and then all of this is history , it takes courage for a seven year old girl to know that beauty is what defines her and it takes courage for a 16 year old girl to tell herself that she would let anything but that define her . So don't preach me about darkness cause I know how it feels , to be an unloved child to be the black sheep of a family to know what innocence will get people through at a very young age , to let your academics define you to a point that failing in it makes you feel less of a human .So don't preach me about darkness cause I have grown from it ,sown from it and I know what it takes, all it takes is courage to be different.

8

Deception

"There is some good in this world and that is worth fighting for" I smiled as I read that quote. Vasco always had a thing about changing my perception of this hopeless world. So much so when he could not be around to nag me with it he got it written on his tombstone. Now every Sunday I visit him. Death made him a good listener I guess otherwise there is no way in hell that Vasco dengluze would not interrupt me midsentence.

I still remember the day as if it was yesterday my first driving lesson he was sitting right beside me on the front passenger seat . I remember every thing our last laugh together , his last words 'You are a horrible driver .I will spare you the details I will spare you the trauma . Just know that after that day Vasco Dengluze was laid to rest and his best friend was the reason he would never walk this earth again.

I ran from my past far to long to tell you this it doesn't leave not until you forgive yourself. And for all the selfish reasons I forgave myself no it wasn't ,

easy but for me it was either that or walking like a half dead person everyday.

And every Sunday I visited him and read him my diary. Just like the old times but now he doesn't make fun of them now he doesn't say my emotions are ever changing .Because Vasco deluze has paid the price of making fun of my emotions.

9

A Girl who was neglected

A dusted glory is all thats left
hearts are broken fears that crept.
When you look back to this there would be nothing left
Minds that are hindered souls that felt .
Longing that searched mocking that look
all that enclosed in a single book .
Of lives lived of people living it and people that would .
Of all should and could and can't and won't
Of the girl you kept behind that bolted door.
Of your existential crisis
Of your never ending banter of what ifs
Of could haves of maybe and of absolutes.

    -The things I found in the eyes of a woman that was neglected

10

Cluster of thoughts

A cluster of thoughts come and go .It would a blessing if I could have jotted each one of them when they were about you . We were the classic unfinished story no matter how good we were it would be the last book a book lover would pick.Some of them say they loved to read tragedies only if they could have read ours .Just like that not a reason known to humanity why you left me . I prayed to god every day that you would be mine , looks like he was in for playing power games because he took you to a better land because he knew you were a better man.

11

Hope

People don't understand the satisfaction you get when you are the only light in someone else's sea of darkness the only thing people wanna clung to when there ship is submerged under water when your the only hope in there hopelessness and the extravegent art in their crooked museum when you are courageous enough to stand by another human being is when you live a life worthy enough to look in god's eye and say you didn't send me over there for nothing Self love is good but we don't realise sometimes it's our excuse to act selfishly.

12

A pill of gratefulness

It's funny how we want everything in our life while some people they just want a day without panic attack , a night without sleeping pill a week without self loathing a month without self harming and it is a prove that how utterly and shamelessly ungrateful we are.

13

Internal wars

They say you live a complete life when you learn how to love the people deep enough to see there suffering as yours , there pain as your pain , there joy as your joy but why , why this life has to always be about them and not me why I am told when I share my pain with others that it is much less than other people and why I am forced to put a smile on my face when I am feeling shitty inside just because our society doesn't accept a person who is depressed and if at all it does why do they have to tell them this thing would fade away with time no it won't it will only grow ,and reach a situation where I don't have an option but to curb everything inside me making concrete wall of pain sorrow helplessness and yet smiling you see because my pain wasn't enough.Enough for them to take it seriously because you see the world suffered world wars and pandemics but I am only suffering because I think a lot or maybe I am too free to think all that shit like stuff bro there are people owning company that are surviving depression and I promise you they have no free time this won't change until we change our perspective on mental health we have to take it seriously ,we might not be going to a battle field

and fighting our asses off but a war within ones own mind
is capable enough to kill him .

14

Raped

For years we kept quite
Just hoping we could see the light .
But today was just not right
A girl who was forever taken from her parents sight .
Cause she took a decision to walk in the dark night .
The demons took away her future which was so bright
And the society thought she could not fight
The judiciary was all in vain
The poor parents could not bear the pain
And we watched it on tv ? and thought it was insane
And for a society we all some how failed
For the politician son was already out
And our judiciary was nothing but a scrout....
And today we must remember the names ,
Because in court it was nothing but a blame game ,
And we thought justice would prevail but those judges they
were all tamed .

15
The last blurb

one day she asked God why you made me so ugly and his only reply was when I created you I thought that it was one of my most beautiful creations and you remain so even if they don't acknowledge it♥?

www.ingramcontent.com/pod-product-compliance
Lightning Source LLC
Chambersburg PA
CBHW061411160726
47995CB00002B/557